Touched by the Infinite Mystery

Touched by the Infinite Mystery

Rockwell Ward

Faraway publishing
Black Mountain, N.C.

Published by
FARAWAY PUBLISHING
125 Spring View Drive
Black Mountain, N.C. 28711
farawaypublishing@gmail.com

ISBN: 979-8-9990731-2-9 (pbk)
Library of Congress Control Number: 2025950563

Printed in the United States of America
10 9 8 7 6 5 4 3 2 1

Cover Photos by Rockwell Ward
All photos by Rockwell and Marrion Ward,
except for "Andromeda" by Tommy Wilkinson

This book is dedicated to my grandparents, Simon and Grace Ward, and my parents, William and Carolyn Ward, who instilled in me a love for storytelling, and to Marrion Ward, my wife and partner in life's journeys for sixty years.

The touch of an infinite mystery passes over the trivial and the familiar, making it break out into ineffable music. The trees, the stars, and the blue hills appear to us as symbols with a meaning which can never be uttered in words.

—Rabindranath Tagore

CONTENTS

PREFACE

My parents and grandparents were storytellers. On summer nights on their front porch, I was enchanted by stories about life on their South Carolina cotton and tobacco farm. My mother, a child of missionaries in Brazil, charmed my brother and me with tales about that exotic country. Dad, a minister, often used stories in his sermons and, during our summer camping trips, enthralled us with happenings from his childhood.

I have carried on the family storytelling tradition by recounting my explorations in caves, outdoor adventures, and travels in various parts of the world. Over the years, people have encouraged me to publish them.

This book, a collection of twenty stories from over fifty that I tell, is a product of their proddings. The stories included in this collection are presented in three chapters. The first is "Above the Earth," in which I speak of the wonder and mystery of the night sky, the amazing discoveries of the nature of the universe, and musings on earthlings' place within the cosmos. A brief futuristic story takes humans to their new home on another planet.

Chapter Two, "On the Earth," includes a mystical experience on a solitary hike in Death Valley National Park. The reader will also meet an angel I encountered on a trail in Washington State. Another story features a trip to the heart of Appalachia with college students, which resulted in an outcome we did not expect.

The final chapter, "In the Earth," offers five stories about exploring wild, noncommercial caves. A close confrontation with death and a mysterious discovery that had been predicted in a dream confront the cavers in the story. There are also moments of encountering the exquisite beauty that can be found only underground. My pilgrimages in the earth revealed the gifts of darkness as well as enhanced the lure of the unknown.

Each chapter ends with a proposed activity for the reader. There is a space for you to record your own personal story on those pages. My hope is that you will be open to beauty, adventure, and challenge. In the process, may you be touched by the infinite mystery.

ACKNOWLEDGMENTS

I would like to thank my wife and adventure partner, Marrion Ward, who has endured the mud and darkness of the caves as well as celebrated the wonders of the sky and the beauty of the land with me. Without her guidance and editing skills, I would never have finished this book.

In addition, I would like to include:

My brother David Ward, who has played a major part in many of the shared adventures in my life.

My daughter Kelly, her husband Charlton Galvarino, and their daughter—my granddaughter—Lily, who have joined me in viewing the night sky, hiking in the woods, and caving explorations.

Bud Fisher, my colleague at Appalachian State University and companion in encountering life's beauty and mystery.

Cavers, including Phil Lucas, Bill Royster, and Gregg Clemmer, who have been partners with me in the challenging darkness of the depths.

Ken Harnage, who composed the Dream Lake Song. Its haunting melody and lyrics still keep me awake late at night.

Ran Shaffner, whose expertise, patience, and generosity were invaluable in helping me bring this book to fruition.

CHAPTER 1: ABOVE THE EARTH

Our feeblest contemplations of the Cosmos stir us: there is a tingling in the spine, a catch in the voice, a faint sensation, as if a distant memory, or falling from a height. We know we are approaching the greatest of mysteries.

—Carl Sagan

THE ECLIPSE

It was a hot, dripping, sticky day on our granddaughter's school grounds outside Columbia, SC. The chili hot dogs and soft drinks had been consumed, and anticipation began to grow among the students, parents, and grandparents. The forecast, a nagging worry of mine, had improved greatly in the previous twenty-four hours, and I began to believe that we just might get to witness the Great American Eclipse.

We were lingering over a Moon Pie in the cafeteria when my daughter Kelly checked her watch and urged us to grab our eclipse glasses, leave the comfort of air conditioning, and start thinking cosmically. Sure enough, once we were outside, eclipse glasses in place, heads raised like sunflowers, we saw the first tiny nick in the edge of the great orange orb of our local star, the Sun.

Lying flat on the ground, we watched in fascination as an ebony, alien object slowly, silently, relentlessly engulfed our luminary. Time passed, but when the brilliant orb was about 80% covered, the light began to change. At first the sunlight seemed slightly less intense, but then the color of the objects on the ground took on an unnatural coppery tone. We could see dozens of mini-eclipses under a nearby tree as the leaves acted as pinhole cameras. The light faded. A cry rang out: "Six minutes until totality!"

I noticed a color gradient in the sky. Close to the Sun, it was still bright blue, but as I looked toward the horizon, there was a range of darkening blue hues in almost concentric circles, unlike anything I had seen before. A cool breeze brushed our faces. The Sun was disappearing fast. Through the eclipse glasses, the little arc of sunlight was shrinking rapidly. The tiny golden crescent shivered for a moment and was gone.

Blackness! Whipping off my protective glasses, I watched in wonder as the final bright flare on the edge of the Moon sparked for an instant and encircled the black obscuring disk with a golden light: the Diamond Ring Effect, and indeed it was! Darkness fell. The cicadas began chirping. The crowd of students and families burst into cheering and clapping as the elusive Corona appeared. Then there was silence.

Silvery, wispy, ghostly appeared that ethereal light like nothing of this world. The corona is the outer atmosphere of the Sun, stretching millions of miles into space but completely invisible except at a special time like this: a total eclipse of the Sun. The sight of that magnificence, the view of that heavenly light moved me and many others from reason to wonder, to tears. Venus scintillated brightly, and the star Regulus shone close to the Moon.

What can be said in the face of such grandeur? The world dropped away, and we stood, transfixed, lifted above ourselves into some other realm, beyond words, beyond thought itself, into a deep and primal connection with something immense and filled with power. The earth moved beneath us, and we felt its orbit.

As I write these words, that numinous feeling stays with me. We are a part of something much greater than we usually realize. We are cosmic beings, citizens of an endless, timeless universe filled with mystery, wonder, and light.

ULTIMATE QUESTIONS

What is our place in the universe? Our neighborhood, astronomically speaking, is made up of our local star—the Sun—and eight planets. These planets are worlds orbiting the Sun and are vastly different from one another.

Looking beyond the planets, beyond the neighborhood of the Sun, we see a sky filled with innumerable stars which are distant suns. This defines the contour of the city of which our neighborhood is a part. We are residents of the Milky Way Galaxy, a huge rotating pancake of hundreds of billions of stars. Our tiny Sun and eight planets are a long way from downtown Milky Way. In fact, the light from the center of our home galaxy takes 26,000 years to reach us. We are definitely in the suburbs!

The cosmos is populated by hundreds of billions of galaxies like the Milky Way. On this scale, the Earth is nothing but a tiny speck of dust drifting in the limitless reaches of infinity.

How do humans on a minuscule world circling a smallish yellow star in a universe of countless galaxies comprehend the immensity of the creation in which we live? Our scientists have created instruments that can study distant galaxies. Through their queries about where we are in the vastness of time and space, astronomers are building a framework for further study. However, limitless questions remain.

Each time a more advanced telescope is invented, additional strange phenomena are discovered. For example, Dark Energy and Dark Matter make up 95 percent of all there is in the universe, yet we understand little about them.

What are humans in the face of limitless time and space? What does it mean that most stars have planets, many of which are favorably positioned for life to be sustained? Will we ever actually travel to the stars, and if so, what will we find?

In addition, what is the meaning of human existence when in a few billion years our Sun will expand and engulf the entire Earth? Our planet and everything upon it will be returned to the stardust from which it was created.

Is it possible for us as a species to learn to appreciate the rich mystery and the beauty of the creation of which we are a part? If so, what would that mean for how we live now and in the future?

THE ARK

My name is Ferdinand, and I want to share with you a few musings from my recent journal entries.

According to my starship's ancient historical archives, the first repeating interstellar SIGNAL was detected by the Green Bank Telescope in West Virginia in what was then called the United States of America, Planet Earth. The date was July 2031.

The SIGNAL was coming from the direction of the constellation Sagittarius toward the center of our Milky Way Galaxy. The reception was clear, but the message was complicated to decipher. It repeated once every seven and a half days, each time adding more information.

The scientific community was reported to be astounded by its complexity, while the Earthlings were overwhelmed by conspiracy theories, which suggested to them that our planet should prepare for an attack by aliens.

As teams of scientists began the task of deciphering the messages, it became obvious that the SIGNAL was of sophisticated design, exhibiting intelligence that appeared to be much more advanced than anything Homo sapiens had acquired.

Our home planet was in chaos. People were questioning: What does this mean? Who or what sent this message?

Should we respond, knowing that a response would indicate exactly where we are in space and time? Or, should we hide in silence?

This mysterious communication was the first realization that other sentient beings were out there in the universe among the stars. As time passed, wars and disputes between the peoples of Earth began to diminish.

Humans banded together with mixed feelings of hope and dread. People all over the world kept looking up at the sky. Should we answer the SIGNAL or keep quiet?

As astrophysicists began to decode the SIGNAL, several findings became evident:

1. We isolated humans are not alone in this vast universe.
2. Beings elsewhere are much more technologically advanced than we are.
3. The Fermi paradox has been resolved.
4. While our planet was on a doomsday path from ecological disaster and continuing war, perhaps an advanced civilization had solved these problems and could offer our world a chance to survive and prosper.

Thus the dream of the great explorers, such as Ferdinand Magellan, Christopher Columbus, Edmund Hillary, and Neil Armstrong, was rekindled in humanity. The idea of a space ship, an exploring vessel, an Ark began to grow.

Meanwhile, the James Webb Space Telescope, the Vera Rubin telescope in Chile, and the span of Earth's array of radio telescopes attempted to pinpoint the exact location of the exoplanet from which the mysterious SIGNAL originated. Finally, they succeeded.

The countries of the world recruited their most qualified technicians, manufacturing experts, astrophysicists, and mathematicians to build the Ark.

The Ark was constructed as a generational ship. Our great-grandparents were the humans who embarked on this momentous journey, knowing that they would grow old and die aboard the Ark. Their ashes would be ejected from the ship into the Cosmos from which they originated. Their children's children would be the ones to arrive at the destination.

From technicians to scientists, linguists to poets and philosophers, a variety of humans prepared for the most ambitious journey humanity had ever undertaken. The Ark was completed, and as the decades passed, it was launched and accelerated toward the infinite.

Those of us on the Ark continue to tell the stories we learned from our forebears about what Planet Earth must have been like. We have never seen a sunrise, smelled the aroma of flowers, dived into a lake or watched deer running across the hills. We have never witnessed a full Strawberry Moon rising above the mountains or gasped at a meteor speeding across a starlit sky. We have never felt the soft, sweet breeze of spring tickle our cheeks and bring a smile to our lips.

All these experiences are meticulously pictured and described in the Ark's voluminous archives, but to us they are nothing more than ancient reflections of a life, a world we voyagers have never known.

Our sterile world on the Ark is made of artificial, mechanical, nonliving materials and machines, which do not stimulate our imaginations like the breezes, aromas, and intense beauty reflected in the work of the ancient terrestrial artists, musicians, and poets.

Thanks to the new invention of the hyper-plasma propulsion system, our Ark has been able to accelerate to a significant percentage of the speed of light. Now, in our manufactured environment three generations later, we are closing in on a giant blue star from whose planet the SIGNAL arrived on our home planet more than 300 Earth years ago.

At this point, communication with Earth is no longer practical. Since we are so far away, a message would take more than 200 years to reach Earth and return to the Ark.

Because of the lack of communication, no one on the starship knows what the conditions on Earth are now.

A few weeks ago, our destination became visible for the first time to the unaided eye. After intense debate on the Ark, we came to consensus that our name for the planet would be Zenathon, which connotes peace and harmony.

As we settled into a low orbit around Zenathon, we stumbled over each other in our excitement to gain access to the Ark's observation portals. We were desperate to get a glimpse of the planet we had studied, dreamed about, and spent lifetimes of light years to reach—our new home.

We shouted to each other about the majestic landscape unfolding below us. One of us described immensely tall crystalline structures dotting the landscape and defying gravity to stretch their gangly arms, twisting toward the sky. Another reported the dance between the azure and deep blue rays of the local star playing on the desert below.

A gasp came from another as she saw the myriad shadows cast by the undulating waves of orange, violet, yellow, and magenta on the surface as they swayed in what must be wind.

Our favorite sight was an expansive light-gray desert sparkling with gleaming diamondlike crystals, spread like marbles strewn across the land.

Now the Ark has left its orbit and nestled into a soft landing on the parched ground. Now we can see distant mountains on the far horizon with an iridescent river meandering through them toward us. This moment is the culmination of humankind's most significant achievement. After a multigenerational journey, we intrepid pioneers, earth's ambassadors, have touched down on an alien world.

WAIT!
Something is coming
Something is coming toward us from across the desert
Getting closer
Our hearts are racing
Here they come
Here they come
We didn't dream of this
We never imagined this
Open the airlock!
Open it!

ANDROMEDA

Who are you, Andromeda?
We glimpse your wispy luminescence at the limit of
    human visibility.
A strikingly beautiful daughter of Queen Cassiopeia,
    we know.
Rescued from the sea monster by Perseus, we heard.
Classified by astronomers as Spiral Galaxy M31,
    we read.

Where are you, Andromeda?
Faintly glimmering so far, so far across a mighty gulf.
Yet we, denizens of your sibling, the Milky Way, are
streaking through the darkness to meet you, embrace
you, and dissolve into you in some unimaginable future
billions of years from now.

What does all this mean, Andromeda?
Your glittering star clouds are spawning worlds
    beyond imagination.
What creatures roam your fantastical shores and look
    our way through alien skies?
Are they, like we, wondering what is out beyond the
    void?

Have you germinated sentient beings who see us
    coming?
Do they know that our galaxy is racing toward your
heart at hundreds of thousands of miles an hour?
Do they understand that we are on our way to
culminate that momentous day when we shall be
    One?

Who are you, Andromeda?
Who are we, essence of the Milky Way?
And who or what shall we together become?

Andromeda, photo by Tommy Wilkinson

OFFSPRING OF INFINITY

To contemplate the cosmos is my daily meditative practice. Each clear night at Starlight Meadows, our farm in Virginia, the beauty of the night sky draws me into a rendezvous with wonder and awe. The Great Globular Cluster is my favorite group of stars to view through the telescope. It leads me to reflect on the fact that we came from the stars.

The elements of our bodies were forged in the immense heat and pressure of exploding stars, called supernovas. In the far distant future when our Sun expands and engulfs Earth, those same elements will be returned to space. We are indeed stardust.

What are the theological implications of such knowledge? Our traditional images and stories have not incorporated this new science. There are at least 200 billion suns in our Milky Way Galaxy alone. Most of those stars have planets. In addition, water, oxygen, carbon, and the other building blocks of life abound in interstellar space. Surely we are not alone.

Who and what are we: bits of stardust in human form? How can our tiny brains comprehend the immensity, complexity, and unfathomable depth of time in which the universe exists? Yet, most of us earthlings simply ignore these mysteries.

It is dangerous to contemplate the Great Globular Cluster in Hercules. To turn a telescope toward it and look back 25,000 years to glimpse the cluster's hundreds of thousands of suns all in a tight multitude is a risky adventure. Why? Because it changes us. Such a journey of the eye and soul might begin to put a different perspective on our place in the universe.

What we understand now about the universe is only a small part of the whole picture. This vastness contains much more that is beyond human comprehension. However, we are an integral part of its composition. That timeless, dazzling immensity is who we are: Offspring of Infinity.

YOUR STORY 1

On a cold, clear winter night, go outside and look up. Take a deep breath, and let the cares of the day fall away. In quietness, absorb the beauty of the stars and planets that illuminate the vast expanse of the night sky. Let this experience draw you into your place in the universe.

Write your thoughts and feelings about your experience in the space below:

CHAPTER 2: ON THE EARTH

And into the forest I go to lose my mind and find my soul.

—John Muir

THE DROP

As the midnight hour arrived, the pickup truck slowed and finally stopped. Silence. The four of us, lying prone under the shell covering the back of the truck, surrounded by all our gear, didn't make a sound. As planned, the driver opened his door, stepped out on the shoulder of the four-lane highway, and raised the hood under the pretense of engine trouble.

Another car flashed past and then three knocks on the tailgate: the "all clear" signal we had been waiting for. As Pete opened the hatch, we piled out with our packs stuffed with technical equipment and 950 feet of climbing rope, connected in two coils because of its weight and bulk.

No words were spoken as we scrambled down the embankment through wet grass and unanticipated briar bushes. Immediately, after we disappeared, the driver closed the hood and drove away across the bridge.

The night was misty with weak moonlight peaking through the fog from time to time. Our helmets were equipped with electric headlamps, but we didn't dare turn them on.

Far below we could hear the treacherous rapids of the New River as it made its way through the gorge. Soon we arrived at a concrete piling. Rebar rungs led us up to a steel platform from which the catwalk stretched out for over 3,000 feet across the abyss. Once on the catwalk, we could see dimly through the mist an endless steel structure of girders and arches, seemingly stretching to infinity.

We walked carefully and slowly on the steel plates of the catwalk. The roadway was about fifteen feet above our heads. Every time a tractor trailer zoomed above us, the whole structure vibrated.

We began looking for a yellow painted spot on the handrail of the catwalk. On a previous trip that had been cut short, we had finally found the right place to hang a rope to avoid the river, power lines, railroad tracks, and trees. On that earlier attempt, daylight was dawning, and we would have surely been spotted on rappel, and police would have been on their way.

When we finally located the yellow mark, we began to lower the heavy rope. The freefall drop would be 860 vertical feet. Anchoring the rope, sorting and adjusting our rappelling gear, double checking each other's rig took quite a while. Time crawled by slowly for me because straws had been drawn on the drive to West Virginia and I had the dubious honor of first on rope.

Breathing shallowly, I clicked the rappelling rack into my harness carabiner, snapped the break bars into place on the rope, and gingerly climbed over the guardrail. Boots planted on the outer edge of the catwalk floor, I leaned back a bit and put my weight on the rope while swinging off the catwalk of the New River Gorge Bridge. Dangling so high above the rocks, a single mistake could quickly end my life.

There is a moment of trust when one must let go of solid protection and put all faith in the fibers of a 7/16"-diameter nylon rope. Taking a last look at my fellow adventures, I spread the break bars on the rack and slowly began my descent into space.

The bottom of the gorge was lost in darkness. The ends of the bridge were invisible. The catwalk and girders above slowly dissolved into the mist as I descended in the clouds. There was a stillness around and within me. After several minutes and perhaps a hundred feet of descent, the world disappeared.

As I glanced upward, the rope dissolved into the moonlit haze. Looking downward, all I could see was a cloud below. The rope was visible for a few dozen feet in each direction before fading away. I tightened the break bars, stopped the descent, and hung in an ethereal space, disconnected from both the structure above and the ground below. It was a magical moment, floating in the mist, with only the distant murmuring of the river as an anchor point.

I don't know how long I hung there. Time was meaningless. As I spread the bars and began sliding down the rope again, for a moment I had the sensation I was sliding almost sideways in the fog. Untethered from both heaven and earth, I drifted in an in-between silvery, vaporous space in which there was no definite up or down, nor was there time and place.

Slowly I spread the bars and became aware of time and gravity as the descent continued.

From below came a distant shout, "Rock, where are you?"

I didn't want to leave the magical clouds of mist, but time was passing, and I needed to clear the rope. Finally breaking through the clouds, I got a clear view of the river far below and the support crew standing by the end of the rope. The bridge above was invisible. Like an alien landing on an unknown planet, I let gravity gently lower me toward the ground.

NIGHTFALL ON MEADOW HILL

Perhaps it was the clear air on our morning hike through the woods to the high pasture. Or maybe it was the sunlight sparkling on the water from the infinite blue of the January sky. Or it could have been the deep, whispering quiet of the eternal hills and deep hollows of that special, secluded part of the landscape of my heart, called Earth Spirit. But certainly what happened on Meadow Hill the other night was yet another glimpse of the mystery of the Presence.

All afternoon I had felt a sense of urgency to get up onto the rocky top of Meadow Hill and watch the sunset. I told Bud that it might be possible to see a thin crescent Moon and a rare appearance of the planet Mercury from the Hill if conditions were just right and if we were lucky.

Chores around the cabin kept me busy as the afternoon hours waned, but in the back of my mind was a strangely insistent urging to climb to the top of Meadow Hill and look to the west for signs in the sky.

For years I have been fascinated by the Anasazi shamans who, from their secluded aeries would watch the skies to determine the intent of the gods. These days, such activities are considered odd at best. However, deep within my archaic being, the urge is still alive within me.

I knew that sunset would be at 5:20, and so by 5:00 my friend Bud and I piled into my old Toyota truck and began the mile-long drive up and out of the Second Creek valley to the high meadows of the Tieche farm. It's amazing how one's perspective changes in that one short mile. Down in the creek valley, the cliffs and hillsides rise steeply, confining the perspective to a limited, secluded horizon. No artificial light is visible from my land, and at times I can live there for days without seeing another human being. The closeness of the land is comforting. Its confining dimensions are finite, known.

As we labored up the steep, rutty road in first gear, we could glimpse the sky through the treetops. It seemed to be clouding up, which was not a good sign. Soon we broke through the end of the forest, passed by the old clapboard house, through the barnyard, and out into the broad field with Meadow Hill ahead on the right. The road consisted of two faint tracks through the pasture.

No words passed our lips. Somehow we knew that this was more than a drive to see the sunset, more than simply moving from one place to another. This was a pilgrimage, a journey of spirit as well as geography.

I turned to the right, out of the field through the gate of the pole barn, yanked the shifter into four-wheel drive, and began the steep, bumpy ascent straight up the side of Meadow Hill. The rough track was punctuated here and there by karst outcroppings of grey, weathered limestone, hinting at the eternal darkness of the caves that lie below.

Then the world began to open up. Like drawing in a deep breath after being underwater, the landscape receded in every direction and fell away below in a magical patchwork of fields, homesteads, ancient rolling hills. In the far distance, high ridges marked the spine of the Appalachians marching down toward the south. On top of the world, or so it seemed, I maneuvered the truck facing southwest, where the golden ball of the setting sun hung like a bright orange pearl over an ocean of greens and blues.

As we stepped out of the truck, I felt a wave of vertigo at the immensity of the scene. Gone was the close familiarity of the hollow below. Here was an endless panoply of intricate, folded geography washing into the shadowy distance.

As the golden globe sank lower, the full orchestra of colors from the deepest turquoise to the boldest red, to the finest filigree of satiny pink, began to infiltrate the sky. Bud expressed the thought that never again would any human witness this exact scene, which was being unfurled before our eyes. We stood in silence, punctuated only by the breeze sighing through the winter grass and the naked limbs of the lone walnut tree that graced the summit.

What can be said in the face of such majesty? So often, as nightfall comes, we turn on the indoor lights, grab the remote to catch the network news, and are oblivious to the grandeur of the glorious close of another day. What cosmic messages are we missing when we concentrate on the frivolous blather of talking heads? The day was complete. The silence and the majesty filled our souls as the melting colors of the sky continued their riotous carnival.

After our mother star had sunk below the far ranges, I pulled out the binoculars to scan the distance. In the deepening twilight, the bands of still-brilliant color jumped closer, and then just on the edge of the field of view, something startling slipped by. I pulled back a bit to the left and felt my breath catch, my pulse quicken.

"I've got the moon," I yelled to Bud. And indeed I had. No more than a whisper-thin sliver of pearly light, the razor sharp crescent was the thinnest I had ever seen. Quietly, shyly it hung there, caught in the act of slipping away in the dusky distance.

Then with a shiver I spotted Mercury, low in a crack between bands of orange clouds, its tiny but piercing searchlight crossing ninety million miles of space to stimulate our optic nerves and send tingles down our spines.

We stood there, two pilgrims on the edge of the world, enthralled as we felt the earth turn, graced by a vision of the Presence of the Mystery—a Mystery so deep we could only stand in silent awe at its arrival. Deep within there was a yearning: a feeling that somehow this was where it all began and where it all ended. We had glimpsed something barely remembered, almost forgotten, but somehow an answer to the wandering, the searching, the endless dance of our lives. A silent whisper of home.

ALONE IN THE DESERT

I was hiking with my brother David in Death Valley National Park, California. The park is a huge expanse of remote, stark wilderness interspersed with hundreds of canyons that are seldom visited. We had been hiking the canyons for days. The silence and solitude were refreshing, a welcome respite from a world of noise and frenzy.

Each day we would hike up a canyon together, exploring the mysteries of the side canyons, climbing the dry falls where we could, and pushing as far as time would allow. Then, as the sun began its decent toward the west, we would turn and retrace our steps down toward the valley floor.

Usually David would start hiking back first. Then, after sitting in silence and solitude for up to an hour, I would begin my own solo journey, following his footprints in the sand. I was conscious of my isolation, and it felt good. I was alone but not lonely. There were no distractions, just the ethereal play of desert light on the multifaceted rocks of the high canyon walls.

The only sound beyond the crunching of my boots in the gravel was the sound of sheer silence. In that deep stillness on the last day in the last canyon, I heard it. Not that I was expecting it, nor was I trying to hear it because it came as a gift.

I heard not spoken words but something clearer than speech, for I heard it in my heart. I heard a Sound that took me beyond myself—the Sound of the crystalline beauty of the Cosmos—and I knew beyond the shadow of a doubt that eternity was near.

APPALACHIAN ODYSSEY

It was a long, hot hike from the debris of the front porch to the cistern. Once there, I knew the pump had to be primed just right to get any water. The priming was a two-handed trick that demanded considerable dexterity. Before the week was over, we had learned to coax at least a little water from that rusty pump. We had also learned the subtleties of an outdoor privy as well. That's not all we learned in the hills of Southwest Virginia in late May. A group of students from Appalachian State University and I labored to build a new porch for folks back in the hills.

As we drove north from Boone toward far western Virginia, there was among us at least something of the feeling that we had the knowledge, skill, background, and money to help the people of Appalachia. That attitude did not last long while we were learning to prime that pump. It soon became evident that the people of Appalachia had much more to offer us than we had to offer them.

They offered us a sense of place, a rootedness and love for the land that most of us mobile city-dwellers had long since lost. They taught us about blood kin, how families stick together and respond to each other in crisis situations. We even began to sense that our hurried, materialistic way of life was perhaps not only unnecessary but not even fulfilling. Standing face to face with poverty, we learned that we often take for granted the abundance we have been given.

We received much more than we gave. While sawing boards, pounding nails, and scraping paint, we remembered that life should not only be focused on the leaders, the rich, the privileged but also on the poor, the oppressed, the sick.

What does a week like that do for volunteers in a strange land? Maybe it will be years before the full change in them comes to fruition. A word, a look, a shared tear may strike a chord, resonate with and change the direction of those people's lives.

A staff member who organized our work stated that his life was changed when he read the appalling contents of a can of potted meat, which was the only meat available in one small store in Appalachia. The injustice represented by that can of beef tripe caused him to give up his middle-class lifestyle with all its luxuries and commit his energy to helping people who were living in the hills.

We left the pump, the newly built porch, the out-of-work family more quietly than we arrived. We left less arrogant but also encouraged, knowing that we had partnered with new friends in Appalachia.

AN UNLIKELY MENTOR

On our land in Virginia, we have created trails across the undulating meadows, through evergreen and walnut forests, and down the hill to the pond. One of our favorite trails leads to Exclamation Point, a high meadow with a magnificent 360-degree panorama of the mountains. We chose the hill's name because invariably, walking through the meadow, we would exclaim in awe as the beauty of the view unveiled itself.

One day, as we were sitting on the grass, feeling the cool breeze and relaxing, we noticed in the distance the top of what looked like an ancient tree with chubby branches laden with abundant leaves and decorated with walnuts. The black walnut tree created a striking scene with billowing white clouds and azure sky as its backdrop.

We could see only the top of the tree because the quarter acre of its realm was littered with autumn olive trees and tall bushes interwoven with wild vines that blocked our entrance to the tree's royal abode. There was no doubt that we would have to clear out those interlopers to free it and allow the tree to stand alone. It would be quite a job, but we were ready to take it on.

For the next year, we recruited any friends and family who visited us to help clear the land. We would all march up the trail to the tree carrying chain saws, nippers, rakes, hoes, heavy gloves, and other utensils of mass destruction.

The job was not an easy one. We would begin by hacking, chopping, or sawing the unwanted trees and undergrowth. As the debris fell to the ground, the tractor gang cut it into manageable lengths to load in the tractor's bucket. Then it was dumped on a secluded part of the land. The pitching crew threw small limbs into the adjoining forest. Then the glove brigade began yanking and hoisting the remaining roots out from their former resting place under the ground.

The day finally arrived when we were going to break through the last part of the undergrowth. We would actually glimpse the mighty trunk that had produced the limbs and leaves with which we had already made an acquaintance. With great anticipation, we separated the screen of bushes and lunged forward toward the tree. What we saw made us gasp.

The bark was peeled back, leaving a two-foot-wide gaping space at the base of the tree. Another tree was growing within that space at the bottom of the trunk. That open space narrowed as it rose twenty feet up the truck to form an elongated triangle. Out from the top of the triangle grew one large limb, bare of bark. It was the ugliest tree we had ever seen. Coupled with that blight were numerous vines that grew from the base of the tree up to forty feet among the branches. Some hung down from the branches like long fake icicles on a Christmas tree.

We, with occasional help from others, had spent countless hours over the preceding year, working at the limit of our ability to clear the land. Our aim to let the tree stand in all its glory in the newly created green space suddenly faded. We had done all that work in vain. The tree wasn't worth the effort.

Giving up is unacceptable to me, so I took pictures and videos of the tree to a friend of mine who knows about trees.

His explanation of the tree's condition changed everything. He determined that the tree had been struck by lightning years ago. That was what began the big split in the bark. What we were seeing now was not a new tree growing inside the old one but the actual core of the tree that was left after the bark was destroyed.

It was the heart of the tree that was visible to us now. Our tree had exposed her heart and even expanded it to grow upward. What courage she had shown. Over the years, instead of wilting and giving up after her former beauty was defiled, she became strong and sent out new branches, leaves, and walnuts. She produced new offspring, two of which lived as healthy saplings near her. She was unable to hide the gouge in her trunk or the loss of her bark, but she remained busy and productive.

Our seeing the essence of the tree and her creativity in dealing with her wound has helped us appreciate the complete tree. Now we greet her with hugs and embrace her external flaws. She has given us the gift of space to contemplate not only our own beauty but to recognize the inherent beauty in all things. Our tree has become an important part, not only of the physical landscape on the farm but also our spiritual landscape as well.

Because he knows this tree is my mentor, Rock provided this space in his book for me to write about her.

—*Marrion*

THE DARK NIGHT

As a chaplain at Appalachian State University, I often took students walking, hiking, and backpacking in the mountains. Late on a Saturday night during a weekend retreat at Montreat, a student suggested we hike up Lookout Mountain.

"Ok," I said, "but let's do something different. Let's walk up the mountain in silence." There was a waning moon that gave a little light, so I upped the challenge: "And with no lights!"

I heard a gasp. Students moaned, "But how can we see the trail? What if we fall down the rocks? We could get lost."

I suggested, "Calm down, and become aware of your senses: sight, hearing, touch, smell, your body moving over the ground. Allow some space between you and the person in front of you. Most of all, pay attention to your emotions, what you are feeling inside." They looked at me like a herd of frightened deer caught in the headlights.

"Are you guys too wimpy to try this?" I teased. And with that, we began our hike.

The farther we walked, we found that our senses became enhanced. There were no lights and no words spoken, but we silently offered hands to each other at the steep places as well as pats on the back and hugs that encouraged the timid to push their limits. While becoming more deeply focused on our inner selves and each other, we also began to pay closer attention to the contours of the rocks. We found that we could learn to see light where before there was only darkness. Somehow personal barriers between each of us were removed, and a deeper sense of belonging to a community and to the earth began to form.

Just last week, I met with a former student, who was passing through Black Mountain. He had been on that dark climb to the mountain top. He talked about how that silent pilgrimage in the moonlight had been a turning point to trusting and sharing in our group and a memory that he will never forget.

THE BURNING TREE

The slanting rays of the autumn sun cast an amber glow on the hilltop as we sat in the green pasture watching the day draw to a close. My friend Bud and I had hiked up the trail in silence, inwardly preparing for our sunset vigil. Perhaps it was the quiet walk, the magnificent autumn splendor, or maybe something else entirely, but we witnessed an extraordinary event that occurred that evening.

As dusk began to descend upon the earth, we left the golden hillside and worked our way down an old, overgrown road sloping through the trees towards Second Creek. The delicious sound of crunching leaves filled my senses until I suddenly noticed a yellow-orange glow filtering through the foliage ahead.

"The woods are on fire!" I yelled breathlessly to Bud, and we began to run. Panting, hearts pounding, we abruptly stopped and stood riveted before an other-worldly spectacle. In a small clearing stood a tall, full Maple tree. And yet, that tree had become something more—much more.

Before our eyes, in the falling dusk, the tree glowed and pulsated with an inner light. It was almost dark now; the oranges, reds, and yellows of the other trees had faded to muted, dull tones. In contrast, before us, light, energy, multicolored radiance, and something else for which I have no words blazed outward like waves of splendor and filled us with speechless awe!

I do not know how long we stood there, spellbound. Time had no meaning in that transcendent place. I remembered the biblical admonition to Moses, "Take off your shoes, you are standing on holy ground."

There were no spoken words, and yet the deepest part of my being was infused with light. A mysterious presence filled the forest. Finally, when eternity had merged again with time, the glow began to fade, and we two wanderers found ourselves standing in the dark woods. No words interrupted the silence between us as Bud and I slowly made our way down the dark hillside, across the low-water bridge over the creek, and finally through the upper field to my cabin.

The next evening, with great anticipation, we hiked back up to the Burning Tree. The tree was there, but it was no different from dozens of others around it: a dull yellow, fading into darkness.

As we stood there in the gathering dusk, I turned my gaze upward toward the stars and realized that, when least expected, the blazing fire of the presence of the infinite mystery does indeed break through and illuminate the darkness of this world.

THIN PLACES

Have you ever stood on a hillside at night far from city lights and found yourself mesmerized by the beauty and mystery of the stars?

Have you ever been in a special place in the mountains or at the seashore where for a few moments the light seemed to change, a certain quietness filled the air, and you realized that you were seeing the familiar in a different way?

While listening to a beautiful piece of music, have you found yourself transported to a different authenticity? If so, you may have discovered a Thin Place.

The ancient Celtic inhabitants of Scotland and Ireland believed that among the mountains and along the rugged coastlines where the wind and waves crashed against the rocks, the membrane between the earthly and the transcendent was thin and porous. These Thin Places seemed to exist in the familiar physical world but also in a different dimension of time and space.

Another way of saying it is that the veil that separates this world from something more is pulled aside. For a timeless moment, it is possible to catch a glimpse of eternity.

Off the western coast of Scotland lies the Island of Iona. It was regarded as a Thin Place by the Celts as well as by recent travelers. Marrion and I found it to be so for us.

Traveling from the mainland to Iona is a pilgrimage in itself.

A ferry leaves from a port in Oban, Scotland, to sail just under an hour to the Isle of Mull. From there, a lovely overland trek across the island reveals misty mountains and shadowy lochs. The crossing takes about thirty minutes and leads to a second ferry that disembarks for a short ten-minute trip to Isle of Iona.

When we arrived on the island, mysterious low-hanging gray clouds and a deluge of rain masked the hills, houses, and historic buildings as we scrambled to our lodging. The relentless pounding of the surf on the island's shores completed the feeling that we were visually and audibly removed from the rest of the world. We were some place special.

The morning brought a clear day, and we set out to explore the rugged natural beauty of Iona.

I circumnavigated the Island following the coast. The beauty of the blue-green water rhythmically lapping against the white sandy beaches instilled in me a deep serenity and peacefulness. In addition, there were rocky cliffs where the waves beat across the granite and the sea birds nested in colonies.

Marrion made a contemplative solo hike down the center of the island on a ridge spotted with heather. She felt the same contentedness as a soft breeze continually kept her company along with flocks of grazing sheep. She enjoyed sitting quietly on the rocks and looking out from the hills to see Iona's place among the other distant islands that dotted the archipelago.

The ancient Abbey, by day or by night, was for us a tangible connection with history and religion. The Abbey's stones held the remembrance of past peoples and holy words. Celts and Scots who traveled there throughout the centuries seemed to hover close by. The evening service in the Abbey was held by candlelight. Dim shadows were cast over the old stone pillars by the soft evening light sifting through the stained-glass windows.

The frantic schedule and noise of our usual days faded on Iona to transform into a time of introspection and connection with its ancient pilgrims. Those seekers had come as we did to marvel in the isle's tranquility and bask in its loveliness. I believe that many of us have had such experiences, however brief. For me, they offer a reminder that there is some larger reality, some greater mystery, some connection with infinity that, when glimpsed even for a moment, can change our life's perspective.

THE MONK

The narrow trail was not marked. When the three of us stepped out of Dave's old Chevy truck, the bracing cold clear air heightened our sense of anticipation. Dave, my younger brother, had suggested that my friend Rip and I might enjoy a hike in the Canadian Rockies to visit a Tibetan monk who lived in solitude in a cave high up in the mountains.

As usual, Dave was not forthcoming with many details in advance. While we put on our hiking boots and filled our packs with warm clothes and snacks, Dave mentioned that actually the trail was rather challenging. Famous for his understatements, Dave had lured me into another one of his wild adventures.

We started out on an uphill track in the forest and after half a mile began to hear the roaring of a mountain river. Rounding a bend, we were confronted with a whitewater deluge growling under an ancient, spindly swinging bridge. Dave casually mentioned that a fall in the river would result in certain death. He wasn't kidding. The huge angry waves, jutting rocks, and the rushing torrent left no doubt in my mind.

Did I mention that my friend Rip is totally blind? Blind but ready for any adventure, Rip's eyeballs had been literally burned in a tragic explosion in the gun turret of a naval destroyer. At six-feet six-inches tall and 250 pounds of solid muscle, Rip is ready for any challenge. He has ski jumped, skydived, caved, and rappelled—all in his total darkness. As we hiked up the mountain, Rip kept his right hand on my left shoulder for guidance.

The spindly swinging bridge did not instill much confidence. Dave, a skinny guy like me, went first.

Then I led Rip to the rusty cables and explained that some of the floor boards were missing. "Piece of cake," Rip muttered as I placed his hands on the cables.

After hiking a couple of miles, the three of us came to a second bridge over the raging torrent. This one was even more intimidating. The boardwalk was not much more than a foot wide. Above was an unstable, sagging cable that offered little confidence. There was no doubt in my mind that Rip could not make that crossing. Dave agreed. We found a place for Rip to sit and told him we would be back in a couple of hours. "Do NOT attempt to cross this bridge, Rip," Dave commanded in a loud voice.

Confident that Rip was settled in a comfortable spot, Dave and I gingerly made our way across the rickety span. From there we could see the cliff face where the monk's cave was located. One final river crossing consisted of two cables only: one five feet above the other. Hooking my boot heels onto the bottom cable and grabbing the top cable with my hands, I wobbled across the abyss, swaying back and forth on loose cables. When Dave arrived, we could still see Rip sitting by the second bridge.

The monk's dark abode lay above. Scrambling up the rocky path toward the cave entrance, I noticed that it was decorated by little painted stick figures of people and animals. At the entrance to the cave was a cord hanging from a bell. At the end of the cord was a hand-written note, stating, "If you wish to speak to the monk, please ring the bell once and wait quietly in silence."

We relaxed, taking in the beauty of the snow-capped mountains. There were no sounds of civilization, no roads or houses visible. The high mountain air, as we inhaled, had a sharp cleanness. This was an untouched wilderness, a place for meditation and peace.

Out of the darkness of the cave, the monk appeared. Dressed in a heavy black cape and hiking boots, he seemed to embrace holiness and practicality. His face was creased from years of rugged weather, but his eyes were bright and alive.

He bowed to us, and we to him. He beckoned us into his cave. In silence we entered his abode. The entrance was about five-feet wide and eight-feet tall. Darkness fell quickly as we left the world behind. Pausing to adapt to the fading light, I noticed a horizontal stovepipe running along the ceiling. As my pupils dilated, I could see a glow coming from within. We entered a wider space and stepped up onto a wooden platform about twelve-feet square. The monk smiled and gestured that we were to sit. His room was lit by a single candle and contained a small desk, a cot, piles and piles of books, and a woodstove that was putting out little warmth. After we were seated on the wooden floor, the monk smiled once more and held his hands in a gesture of prayer.

We sat in silence by the light of the candle. My back was against the rock wall of the cave, and as time and silence engulfed us, I began to feel the energy of the glacial river vibrating the rocks. It was like a low-voltage electrical current tickling my spine.

I lost track of time and space in the womb of the mountain. The cold air, the solid rock, the flickering candle, the moan of the water below—all were a cleansing, purifying gift.

Finally the Monk stirred, lit a kerosene lamp, and invited us into conversation. He told us that he had lived in the grotto for almost twenty years. About every two months he walked down the mountain to obtain supplies. Usually he would repair the bridges but stated that he wanted the path to remain a challenge to discourage all but the most determined seekers.

After giving us his blessing, we walked to the entrance and full daylight. Dave mentioned that we had brought a blind man with us who wanted to ask a question. However, as I looked across the gorge toward where we had left Rip, my heart skipped a beat when I realized that he was not there. Dave gasped, "Oh, NO!"

Then we spotted him at the cable crossing. He had navigated the second bridge: alone and blind!

The Monk accompanied us across the cables to where Rip was sitting. I was angry but also thankful. Rip was a wild man that could not be tamed.

Dave explained that the Monk had come to answer Rip's question. But first, the Monk, gazing into Rip's artificial, painted eyeballs, asked incredulously, "You are a blind man, and you came all the way here?"

Rip shared a bit of his life of darkness with the Monk, acknowledging that he struggled with his handicap and was depressed about his future. The Monk asked if he had a spiritual life. Rip answered that he did not.

They talked a bit longer, and then the Monk put his hand on Rip's shoulder. We all stood in silence for a few minutes.

What the Monk said then I will never forget:

**"Beware of those who have all the answers.
Do not be afraid of darkness.
An encounter with God can be both scary and
dangerous."**

Bidding farewell to the Monk, the three of us slowly made our way down the mountain trail, crossed the challenging bridges, and as the late afternoon sun began to fade, I pondered the meaning of his enigmatic words. As I write these words many years later, I continue to reflect on his cryptic advice.

ANGEL ON THE TRAIL

I never really believed in angels. That is, until the day I met one! Here is how it happened.

I was in Washington State and was looking forward to a day of solitude, hiking in the high mountains of North Cascades National Park. I parked my brother's old Chevy truck at 8,000 feet where the gravel road meets the Pacific Crest trail.

The brilliant, snow-clad peaks cut the deep azure sky like the teeth of a ripsaw. I could see for a hundred miles as the trail knife-edged around the slopes. I walked in solitude for a couple of hours, then paused on a rock by a field of snow to eat a snack lunch. I knew I was alone since there had been no other cars at the trailhead.

Needing time to reflect, I wanted to to get away for a while and relax. I finished my snack and resumed my journey. As often happens when hiking, I thought about my life: where I had come from and where I might be going.

Lost in reverie, I was caught by surprise when a voice close-by said, "Hello!" Sitting on a rock above the trail was a little old lady dressed in a pink jacket and black hiking pants. In her hand was an ancient walking stick that had seen its share of mountain miles.

"Where are you going?" she asked.

"Probably not much farther," I answered, realizing that it was now mid-afternoon.

"Well," she said, "you could leave the trail, climb that ridge to the left, and have a great view as you cut back toward the trail on which you just came."

Squinting up at the ridge against the sky, I realized to climb would be a challenge. I had no ice axe, no crampons or rope. A bit intimidated, I asked, "Think I could make it up there?"

"I'm sure you could make it," came the reply. "Wave when you get to the top."

The ridge was a rocky crag. There were pockets of snow and ice as well as deep drop-offs on each side. As I worked my way higher, to my dismay the ridge climbed almost straight up to a knife-edged spire of rock, two feet wide and 200 feet long, ending in a grassy knoll perched beyond the abyss.

Looking down from where I had come, I could make out the bright pink jacket among the rocks hundreds of feet below.

I waved my hat and thought I could hear a faint, "Well done!" But maybe it was just the keening of the wind.

As my gaze swung back to the thin blade of rock before me, I felt my stomach lurch and the blood pound in my ears. To the left, the drop-off was hundreds of feet to an almost vertical snow bank.

The right was just as bad with dozens of feet of free-fall to a nasty scree slope dropping away into a steep valley thousands of feet below me.

I could not do it! Without a belay, a safety rope, I wouldn't dare crawl across that chasm. But I couldn't go back down and face the cheerful pink lady either! She said I could do it.

Instead of climbing the rest of the way up to the beginning of the knife-edged ledge, I gingerly eased to the right, hugging the base of the rock spine and treading lightly on the unstable shards of the scree slope.

When the second handhold had broken off and I heard the rocks dislodged by my boots crashing down into oblivion, the dry taste in my mouth made me face the fact that I could die here, and soon.

It was then that I heard a noise above me. Slowly I looked up, and there she was, hands in pockets, walking along that narrow blade of rock, fifty feet above my head!

"What are you doing down there?" she asked. "You'll do better up higher," her amused words drifted down.

I held on, forced my breathing to slow, and carefully backtracked the way I had come to the climb up to the knife edge. Slowly, ever so slowly, I eased myself out onto that sliver in space.

The wind moaned, the earth turned, the peaks rose and fell like breakers in the blue. I breathed in and out, heart galloping, time slowing; one hand, then one knee moving; the emptiness on each side calling my name.

As if in a dream, I focused in the shimmering distance on the grass-covered peak with the flash of pink: Paradise. Then, somehow, I was there, crawling, hugging the earth, my gaze slowly rising to infinity.

There were never-ending peaks like billows of clouds everywhere, as far as the eye could see.

I soaked in the silence, the warmth of the sun, the faint and the far-off melody of creation itself.

Raising her arms in a gesture of awe that encompassed all that we could see, she simply smiled, a deep, wise, knowing smile. No words were necessary. Words would have profaned the majesty that engulfed us.

For time beyond time, we simply sat and drank in the beauty and the wonder. It felt like a warm gush of water: peace and a deep joy rushed into my being. Here was a glimpse of the Garden of Eden. Indeed, God was walking with us here.

"I'll be going now," her words broke the silence. I looked up as she stood and headed over the crest, away from the rock spire, towards a long, sloping meadow that met the trail far below.

Walking away, she paused and looked back. Again, that enigmatic smile washed over me, and she was gone.

I sat transfixed by the symphony of wilderness playing around and within me, knowing that something rare and powerful had touched the depths of my soul. After a few minutes I stood and walked to the edge of the mountain's shoulder. I could clearly see the trail a good half-mile below and all the sloping meadow leading down to it.

In fact, I could see the trail at least a mile in each direction. It was empty. There was no one in sight, anywhere.

The late afternoon breeze ruffled my hair as I raised my arms, embracing creation, for then I realized what I had somehow known inside. I had been in the presence of an angel, a messenger from God who came to me and said three things I will never forget:

Where are you going?

What are you doing down there?

You'll do better up higher.

I believe that there are messengers from the universe all around us. Most of the time we forget to open our eyes or our ears or our hearts to be aware of them. They are here, whether on the trail or at our workplace or in the quietness of our room at night. They are here.

YOUR STORY 2

On a warm spring afternoon, take a walk in the woods. Feel the softening earth beneath your feet. Notice the new buds forming on the trees and flowers. Breathe in the scent of the woods and the new life forming there.

Write your thoughts and feelings about your time communing with nature in the woods:

CHAPTER 3: IN THE EARTH

The cave you fear to enter holds the
treasure you seek.
                                    —Joseph Campbell

THE ETHEREAL LIGHT

In a dark time, the eye begins to see.
—Theodore Roethke, *Julian of Norwich*

It started raining Thursday afternoon before Matt and Shawn arrived. That night, as I lay in bed mentally preparing for the caving trip the next day, I was at first lulled by the steady drumming of the rain on the tin roof. As the hours slipped by, the downpour did not stop but grew only stronger, and I began to worry. Would the road out from the cabin be flooded, or, worse yet, would there be too much water in the cave? Morning proved that the creek was indeed rising, at least a foot up from the night before, and it was still raining.

When we arrived at Organ Cave, I was amazed to see how much water the enormous entrance was taking. The owner had real misgivings about our entering but trusted my judgment. After putting on all our gear, trying to stand under the back liftgate of my truck to stay dry, we entered the cave, descending the stairway into the huge Chapel Room.

At the end of the commercial walkway, we turned into a side passage, sat awhile in the dark, and I led the three of us in a preparatory meditation to let go of the things of the surface and journey into the darkness of the cave and into our inner beings.

At the end of the tourist trail, we ducked under the guardrail and stepped into the muddy, rushing water. The first twenty minutes were not difficult. We found rocks jutting out of the water, so we could hop from one to the other and stay dry. However, I was concerned about something else. Soon in the distance we could hear a mighty roaring. Flowing over Ten Foot Waterfall,

all the surface water from the entrance was pouring into our passage with a deafening, thunderous blast.

Below that point the fifty-foot-wide passage was filled with a series of rapids, small falls, and, as we peered into the darkness beyond, a mind-numbing din.

My better instincts were yelling at me to 'turn back now!' But something else led me to try the first crossing. The current was strong and the footing uncertain. I knew if we could make it down to the Discovery Passage, a hole high up on the left-hand wall, we would be above and out of the water. We finally made it to the opening, though the last two crossings were difficult due to the depth of the water and the tugging strength of the current.

Deep down inside me, the old fear of drowning in a cave was beginning to surface—taking me back so many years to that night of hell in flooded Fullers Cave when we had given up all hope of getting out alive.

But when the three of us finally climbed up into the Discovery Passage, it was dry and quiet! The absence of sound was comforting, like a soft blanket gently laid over us. So we agreed to travel in silence, without talking. Passing through the T-Room, the A-Trail, and the Throne Room, we began our long trek south, down the Upper Stream Passage toward our distant destination: the Waterfall Room.

I was glad that we were only three and that we were not carrying on the usual chattering that goes with caving. I found myself listening to the cave and hearing little trickles of water here and there that I knew were not usually present. I listened to the Silence, and it was good!

Finally, in the dark distance, we could begin to hear, or actually feel, a deep throbbing of pounding water in the Waterfall Room. I knew it would be impressive—the cathedral-size room has two fifty-foot waterfalls peeling off a high ledge. Usually they are only a trickle or a shower, but today . . . .

Matt and Shawn had never been there and were as keyed up with anticipation as I was. As we drew nearer, the deep pounding became palpable. The air was vibrating with ferocious power. The energy in the cave was dynamic. Matt had wanted to lead part of the trip, so I decided to let the two of them explore the Waterfall Room on their own.

We climbed up a twisting passage with lots of rushing water, ducked under a ledge, and looked up. To my right, one of the falls was hitting the rocks, and the mist and spray made the higher reaches of the room invisible. Talking was out of the question, so I ducked back down and motioned them to go on and climb up the massive rock pile to the top of the room. We had already agreed that I would retreat down the passage a little way and wait while they explored on their own.

And so I backtracked, happy to have some alone-time and feeling good at how excited they were to explore something without having to follow me. I figured they would be gone an hour or so, so I found a comfortable gravel bar to wait on, put down my ensolite pad to sit on, took off my helmet, and put on a nylon hat for warmth. Thus settled, I reached over and clicked off my headlamp.

Ah, the instantaneous blackness—darker than the darkest night but, after all these years of caving, an old friend. Instead of the utterly silent stillness of dark that

I am used to in caves, the air was alive with the energy of rushing water. The small stream where I sat was gently gurgling, and I could hear it pouring over some rocks as it disappeared into a hole in the floor. Underlying all of this and seemingly surrounding me was the pulsing deep-base note of the mighty falls in the Waterfall Room above. It was as if the air itself were dancing, as though the rocks themselves were awakening from their timeless slumber.

As I sat there in the eternal night, a smile crossed my lips. There was indeed a majesty and a Presence here, like never before. And then, in the midst of all that glorious sound—from the deepest, gut-felt throbbing to the highest treble hiss of seething liquid—I began to see it. Creeping in from the edges of my peripheral vision, it appeared. Subtle, wispy, ghostly, it appeared: a greenish blue Ethereal Light. Not that I could focus on it. Not that it appeared as a solid thing or a distinct image but a warm, enveloping glow. And with that heavenly light, a sense of deep peace and joy stole over me—sitting there muddy and wet, hundreds of feet below the surface of the earth, in a dark flooding cave; and yet I knew, somehow, that "all shall be well, and all shall be well, and all manner of things shall be well."

STUCK

In a recently discovered cave in western Virginia, the possibility of exploring a new passage had been created. A group of cavers from Richmond had pushed into a remote area of the cave until they were finally stopped by a large boulder blocking a crawlway opening. Water was flowing from beyond the rock, and fresh air was blowing out. Guaranteed virgin passage was waiting to be discovered. A Vietnam vet in our caving club, an explosives expert, joined us on that trip. He rigged a charge of dynamite to demolish the impassable rock.

The cavers scrambled out of the way and disappeared around a couple of corners before the blast was detonated. Dust and toxic fumes from the explosion kept the cavers from going back to see if the rock had been destroyed.

Two weeks later, my brother Dave and I were able to join the group to see if we could push past the demolished boulder and discover new passages. We were excited but realized that this would be a strenuous adventure.

About two hours from the entrance was the infamous Pants Off Crawl. Three of us were skinny and could probably squeeze through the Crawl. The others were larger so they had to take the longer route through neck-deep David's Lake.

Pants Off was no picnic. It was only ten-inches-or-less high but about three-feet wide. The way to slither into its funnel was to lie on your belly, push your helmet ahead of you, and strap your cave pack onto one foot to drag it behind. Next you had to be sure to turn your head to the right. As I started the crawl, the rocks pressed close and tight. I could feel my heartrate accelerating. The passage led down hill and was about ten-feet long.

I assumed that after the crawl, we would again be in walking passage. No such luck. The cave passage was small and wet. Only 15-to-20-inches high, it was filled with several inches of cold running water. We were wearing dry suits under our coveralls, but that slither was an ordeal.

Finally we arrived at the junction where the boulder had been dynamited. The David's Lake cavers were there waiting for us and wondered why it had taken us so long to arrive. We growled at them. We had brought a couple of army surplus trowels, which made digging the debris from the shattered rock easier.

Beyond, the undiscovered blackness beckoned. That passage was also barely tolerable. It was several feet wide and filled with a viscous mix of mud and water. We pushed, crawled, and breaststroked through the deep muck. We had actually thought this adventure was going to be fun!

Eventually we came out into a large room with gleaming formations and tantalizing passages fanning off in different directions. After enjoying the thrill of discovery, we made a quick survey and sketch of the area with paper and pencil. Then we headed back toward the distant entrance.

Dave, Rick, and I reentered the dreaded tunnel toward Pants Off Crawl. We were getting tired, and that made it feel like a much longer trip to get back to the Crawl. Dave and Rick squeezed through the tight pinch, and then it was my turn. I wasn't looking forward to forcing my way into the slot. I was in a hurry to get it over with. I felt the pressure of tons of rock over my back, and the rough surface beneath me was grinding into my gut. Then I realized with a gulp that I was stuck. Stuck—wedged tight in a crack hundreds of feet below the surface of the earth, pinned like a dead moth on a display board.

Dave yelled into the slit, "What's holding you up?"

My response is not printable. Attempting to assess the situation, I quickly realized that since I had turned my head to the right coming in, I should have turned it to the left going out. I could not move an inch forward or backward, nor could I draw a deep breath because of the pressure of the rocks on my chest and back.

I remembered the old advice for stuck cavers is to relax: not to struggle or be frantic because that tenses the muscles, increases the blood pressure, and wedges the body even tighter. I tried to follow that sage advice but did not succeed for long. In addition, the flame on my miner's carbide headlamp was dying down. The muddy trio arrived from the direction of David's Lake and began to assess the situation. I could hear the mumble of their voices from my rocky entombment.

My brother squeezed in toward me, grabbed my right hand, and pulled hard until I yelled. I was afraid he would dislocate my shoulder. I could not take a deep breath because my chest was being squeezed. Then the creepy fingers of fear began to crawl up my spine. I couldn't back out. I couldn't inch forward. There I was, stuck hundreds of feet below the surface and hours from daylight and freedom.

I lost all track of time. Finally my brother had a creative idea. He stripped off his coveralls and somehow contorted his body so that he could reach the waist of my coveralls. He grabbed the fabric and after several attempts was able to slide me over about an inch. Then another inch and another. Then he could pull me forward, inch by inch, until I was free.

Prone on the mud and released from hell, I lay there panting, completely drained and exhausted. We were two hours from the outside, mostly uphill including a thirty-foot vertical rope assent. With ebbing strength, I was finally able to reach the entrance. While I don't remember anything about the trip out to the warmth and sunlight of late summer, I have to admit that I will never forget the relentless clutches of Pants Off Crawl.

ALL HOPE LOST

On a bright, crisp spring morning many years ago, four of us entered Fullers Cave. It was not a tourist cave, like Luray Caverns or Carlsbad. There were no walkways, no handrails, no guides, no electric lights to illuminate the path, just rocks and mud and darkness and water, lots of water.

We had been exploring and mapping caves for years, but this one was a difficult and dangerous challenge. My brother Dave, Bill, Gene, and I left the sunshine and spring flowers behind, climbed down a remote sinkhole in the woods, and entered a narrow canyon passage. Twenty to forty feet above our heads, logs were wedged across the canyon, evidence of the periodic massive flooding, which would be deadly for anyone trapped within the cave. The weather report called for sunny skies, but it was April.

Properly equipped, we wore drysuits under our coveralls and helmets with carbide miner's lights. Our packs contained extra sources of light, food, and first-aid supplies along with ropes and climbing gear for the three waterfalls down which we had to rappel, more than a mile from the entrance.

Hours later, below the waterfalls, we executed a technical climb up a canyon wall and found several thousand feet of virgin passage. We stood in awe at a passage where no human had ventured before and where no light had ever shone. This type of discovery is a caver's ultimate dream.

When we finally headed back upstream toward the waterfalls, we were shocked to see that the amount of water had increased dramatically. The raging torrent extinguished our lights and battered our bodies as we struggled to ascend the ropes through the falls. It was obvious that the cave was flooding.

About an hour above the waterfalls, we encountered my worst nightmare. The way out toward the entrance of the cave was a long, low crawlway, and it was completely filled with churning, muddy water.

There was no way through. There was no passage to lead us to light and hope and springtime and life.

Our eyes reflected the despair we all felt. We were trapped, penned in, cut off from the everyday world, with no means of communication to report our dire situation. The fear of death crept through our veins.

What could we do? We could not turn around and go back to the lower level from which we had just come. The flood would fill that part of the cave first.

In the roaring darkness, Bill spoke first. "I was once told," he said, "that if you are ever caught in a flood in Fullers Cave, try to find the SSS entrance."

"So where is this entrance?" somebody yelled.

There was silence among us. We all looked at Bill. There was a long pause.

"I don't know," he confessed. He finally answered over the din of the raging water, "As I recall, someone told me that the junction toward the SSS entrance is a climb up on the right-hand wall of this passage and back down between here and the top of the waterfalls."

"That is several thousand feet, going back deeper into the cave!" I screamed.

He yelled back, "What's the alternative?"

We slowly began backtracking down toward the waterfalls, checking the right-hand side of the passageway, waste deep in the plunge pools, as the relentless force of the rushing current threatened to wash us away. We climbed into several cracks in the walls of the passage, but all of them led to dead ends.

Time passed, but for us it was swept away in a torrent of fear and despair. Finally, at long last, Gene spotted another crack in the limestone and forced his way through until he disappeared. We all stopped.

He came back and announced, "I think this just might be the way!"

As we made our way through a narrow sinuous slot, the tumultuous sound of the flood gradually faded. I could breathe again and feel the terror slightly diminishing. Before long we began to hear water ahead, and we encountered another rushing torrent coming toward us. The passage was two to six feet wide and trending steeply upward. There were a series of waterfalls four to fifteen feet high that we had to chimney up and climb over. Gene lost his footing and washed over one of the smaller falls. The flame of his carbide lamp was immediately extinguished. Luckily Bill was downstream and grabbed him as the current attempted to wash him away into the maw of darkness.

Time had no meaning in that black, treacherous canyon. Finally, we were able to climb out of the slot and up to a wide, muddy room about thirty feet in diameter but only four-feet high. From a two-foot-wide crack in the middle of the floor, the flood dragon intensified his bellowing rampage.

Shining our lights around the open space, someone noticed a small opening in the wall opposite where we were sitting in gooey mud. Gene jumped across the deep crack and crawled into the hole. Soon we saw his boots appear as he backed out. "No go," he said. "It goes ten feet and stops at a dead-end wall."

No way out! We were trapped like rats in a flooding sewer.

Just a year before, six cavers had died in a flooding cave in New York State. When their bodies were finally recovered, the tips of their fingers were bloodied to the bone as they clawed the ceiling when the last inch of air space disappeared. We all knew about that horrible drowning since the caving chronicles had extensively covered the tragedy. We began to realize that the same fate might extinguish our lives, but we didn't dare talk about it.

The deafening torrent in the crack in the floor of our miserable mud cell seemed to be growing louder and closer. We sat there in the dark, the cave filling with water, and I knew I was going to die. There was no way out, no one to rescue us. All hope was gone.

My life passed through my mind in technicolor as I sat in the dark, dank alcove. I saw scenes of my childhood, teen years, and college graduation. The part that was the most agonizing was my upcoming wedding to Marrion in fewer than two months. It would not take place. In addition, my parents would be devastated by the loss of their two sons.

Hours passed. We sat there, each with his own cherished memories and fears of what we had yet to face in the cave. Finally, we extinguished our carbide lights to conserve fuel, though none questioned what difference it would make. Time lost all meaning. There was only the stygian darkness and our combined fear. How would we react when the water finally came for us?

We sat and waited. We stretched our arms and legs and waited.

The water continued to rise. We waited.

Suddenly, out of the blackness and the roar of the water came Gene's unexpected howl. I thought he had panicked. I lit my carbide lamp and panned it across our limestone prison to where he was continuing to yell. Suddenly I realized what he was saying.

"I smell grass, I smell grass!" With that he disappeared into the tight hole he had declared a dead end hours earlier.

The remaining three of us grabbed our packs, put on our helmets, and followed him. It began as a tight belly crawl that made a right angle turn in about ten feet. It looked like a dead end, but I too could smell the sweet, fresh April grass. It was a squeeze, but we popped out under a small ledge into a pasture.

What a glorious vision! Off to the west, there was the waning gibbous Moon hovering over the black cloudbank of the receding storm. I rolled over on my back, and there majestically floating above me was our Galaxy, the Milky Way, filled with innumerable welcoming stars.

Lying there on the ground, gasping, with my feet barely out of the flooding abyss, I watched the moonlight illuminate the raindrops on the grass. It was as if a million diamonds had been strewn wildly across the field. It was the most beautiful sight I had ever seen. I had seriously awaited my death, lost all hope, and now my brother, my friends, and I were alive. Alive! We had no idea where in the countryside we were, but it didn't matter. We had survived!

The miracle of our escape from the flood continued when, several months later, the part of the cave that had been our refuge was fully mapped. The survey revealed that the passage from the Fullers stream where we had started our harrowing trip to safety, leading to the SSS exit, does not exist. There is no passage there.

No way through! There was nothing but solid rock, although, somehow, for us there *was* a passage—a passage to safety and to life. Life!

GLIMPSES OF ETERNITY

Our footsteps echoed like a slow drumbeat off the cold rock walls. Our lights pierced like tiny needles into the vast darkness that seemed to have no end. Something pulled us deeper, farther and farther away from that tiny passage which had led us in from the light and air and sky. The depths called us inward toward the unknown.

It had been a rough few weeks. The students were stressed out as the end of the semester approached, and I found myself preoccupied with the pressure of my own schedule. A caving trip for the weekend with several students seemed like a good idea. It was a chance to get away and blow off a little steam.

This cave was different from most of the others we had explored together over the years. It had recently been discovered, and few people had been there. In fact, only one other group had ventured into the remote passage we planned to navigate on this trip.

Nothingness loomed ahead as we approached a huge, black junction. Off to the left in the distance, we could barely make out arching rock ceilings as the passage bore down into the mountain. However, we chose the right-hand fork and began to pull ourselves over huge fallen boulders. Hours passed. It was time to head back, and most of it would be an uphill pull.

Then we spotted it. At the top of a flowstone wall was a small opening. The unknown darkness of that hole beckoned seductively. What lay behind that entrance? Had any humans ever passed that way before?

Slipping and clawing for handholds, like spiders we inched our way up that wet, muddy rock face. The opening was just above us. We could not see what lay beyond. Taking the lead, I pulled myself up the last few feet until my face was level with the passage. As the beam of my headlamp illuminated the eternal blackness, my mouth flew open in an involuntary gasp. Unimaginable wonders lay before my eyes. In all our years of caving, none of us expected anything like the spectacle before us.

A hushed silence fell over us as we carefully crawled into this chamber of treasures. Weird yet exquisitely beautiful formations filled the passage. Scintillating in the lamplight were arches and pillars of pure white calcite, which seemed to defy the laws of gravity. Many of the slender columns were leaning as though an unseen hand had slowly pushed them aside for thousands of years. In places, even the floor was completely covered with gleaming white crystals.

Soon we ran out of words to express our amazement and delight. We just sat silently drinking in the unearthly beauty. The silence was so deep I could hear the blood coursing through my temples. Alive in every sense of the word, totally absorbed in what we were experiencing, we were in flow. Time stopped. We became a part of eternity.

I do not know how long we sat there. For me, it was forever or only an instant. The world faded away, and a sense of peace and deep joy, like a pulsing blue light, filled my being. It was as if I were waking up and realizing that for most of my life I had been asleep.

Has this ever happened to you? Not necessarily in a cave but perhaps when you were walking outside, after hard hours of concentration, to find the sky filled with innumerable stars. The feeling of the immensity and unspeakable beauty of the universe is over-whelming. Maybe it has happened in the silence of a walk in the woods when suddenly the sunlight grows clearer, your eyesight sharper, your body suddenly alive and awake. Perhaps you have experienced it in listening to music or in deep, honest sharing with a friend. These moments may be brief and rare, but somehow in these timeless interludes, we are touched by awe and wonder. Our body, mind, and spirit are filled with a light and a peace vastly different from the ordinary.

In these eternal moments, we find ourselves in the presence of a reality beyond the usual boundaries of time and space. While for most of us these glimpses of eternity are fleeting, we never completely forget them. We have been touched by the eternal mystery, and somehow we know deep down inside that we are loved and that there is no longer any need to be anxious, lonely, or afraid.

DREAM LAKE

Abandon hope, all ye who enter here.
—Dante, Inferno

In West Virginia, up on the side of a mountain, a stream cascades down the rocks, falls over the lip of a sinkhole, and disappears into the darkness of Fullers Cave. Four of us in our mid-twenties had been exploring the cave often for two years. We had almost died in a flood there months earlier, but we kept coming back. There was something about this particular dark, yawning opening that called us to venture into the unknown.

On this return trip, after rappelling down the three waterfalls and over a mile from the entrance, several of our team of cavers reached what we all had thought was the end of the cave. It was a place where a big passage was blocked by a rockfall that had taken place years before. Huge boulders had completely sealed off the passage.

Bill, kneeling in a stream with his face close to where the water flowed under the rock, felt a breeze blowing toward him. This could only mean there was air space leading to whatever lay beyond. In his wetsuit, he lay on his back in the stream. He took off his helmet and his pack and dragged them behind him. With his shoulders, he grooved a trench in the gravel which enabled him to slide slowly under the rocks. He found about an inch of air space with his nose scraping along the rocks above. Gasping, he expected the air to run out at any moment.

Just the opposite happened when suddenly he realized there was nothing above him now except blackness. No mud-covered boulders. He pulled himself out of the stream and relit his light. He saw a passage that bore down into the mountain.

Breathless with excitement, he yelled back to the other guys, "Come on! Come on!" As they followed him through, their hearts racing, they discovered several thousand feet of virgin cave.

After a long trek of climbing up and down mud banks and wading through a stream, they could hear a roaring in the distance. Around a bend, they saw nothing ahead except a tremendous blackness that their lights could not penetrate. As they walked out from their passage that was 25-feet high and 25-feet wide, they were engulfed by an enormous emptiness with a river flowing right in front of them. Wading across the river, they climbed up a huge steep mud bank on the other side.

From there, even with the aid of their lights, they could not see the far side of the room, nor could they see the ceiling. They had never been anywhere like this under the ground, and they had never even heard of a room that big in a cave. More importantly, they knew they were the first to discover it.

Even though they were completely ecstatic about their discovery, they realized they had already been underground many hours and knew they had to head back. They had marked their path up the huge mud mountain, so they followed that path down and waded back across the river.

Next came the little stream they had followed into the new discovery, and they began to make their way back into the passage that had earlier seemed large but now seemed insignificant. After slithering under the rocks, they jumarred up the three waterfalls and began the long trudge toward the distant entrance.

When they got home that Sunday night, I got a call from Bill. He was so excited he could hardly talk. He meticulously retold the story of their trip and what they had found. Immediately, we planned a trip for a month later to go back to that huge mud mountain in the big room and head downstream in the river to see what we could find. We knew we had one of the biggest finds in West Virginia. It was an incredible cave, but we had no idea what we would discover on our next trip. I had trouble falling asleep that night, filled with anticipation of what was to come.

We prepared to leave Richmond on a Friday evening to head to West Virginia and enter the cave on Saturday morning. We planned for a twenty-hour trip. Paul had been on the previous trip when the big room was discovered, but he couldn't go on this trip. Bill had gone to Paul's house to get some extra equipment, and he was putting it into the back of his station wagon and getting ready to rush out to meet the rest of us.

Paul called out, "Bill, before you go, I've got to tell you what happened."

Bill responded, "I haven't got time. I've got to go meet the rest of the guys. We wish you could go with us, but we've got to get going so we can get up there before too late tonight. We need to get some sleep so we can be ready to go in the cave tomorrow."

"Something happened last night," Paul said. "You need to to know about this, Bill."

Bill sighed, "Okay. I've got to go, but tell me what happened."

Paul began, "I had a dream about that cave."

Bill complained, "Good grief. I haven't got time for dreams. What are you talking about?"

Paul answered, "It was unlike any dream I have ever had before, and I need to tell you before you go."

"Okay. Okay. Tell me while I'm throwing this stuff in the car."

Paul's Dream

It was more like a vision than a dream. In this nightmare or whatever it was last night, I found myself standing in the big room we had discovered. I was alone. I was standing on the edge of the stream in my wetsuit, and I could feel the water tugging at my legs. I could feel the helmet on my head. I knew that the purpose of the trip was to go downstream to see what we could find. Even though I was alone, I started off heading downstream, following the edge of the river.

Sometimes I was in the water, sometimes on the bank, and sometimes clambering over boulders. I came to the end of the big room, and I was in a tremendous passage I estimated to be a hundred feet across with a river flowing down the middle of it. I followed that passage.

It went around a bend to the right and then a bend to the left. As I walked along, I thought it would go for miles and miles.

Suddenly I went around a bend, and the passage ended in a lake. I didn't expect that. I could see by shining my light around that the lake had no opening at the end. The ceiling was flat about ten feet above the water. It was very wide, and the sides curved out and dropped straight down into the water.

79

I could see no opening, yet the river flowed into the lake. Floating on the lake was a yellow foam about a foot thick in places. As I stood there looking at it, I began to get upset. I grew more and more agitated because I knew something was wrong. There was something evil about this place, something terrible, something like death.

Thank goodness, I began to wake up from this dream, this vision, this nightmare. But before I could wake up completely, I looked down and found myself standing in the middle of the river on a sandbar shaped like a crescent moon. With that, I woke up, covered with sweat, shaking from head to toe. Needless to say, I didn't sleep at all the rest of the night because it wasn't even like a dream. It was like I was there. I was really there!

Bill reacted dully. "Well, that's really something, Paul. Unfortunately, I've just got to go."

Bill jumped in the car and took off. He met us half an hour later, and together we carpooled on our drive to West Virginia. The four of us camped at Greenbrier State Forest, which is about ten miles from the cave, and were eaten up by mosquitoes all night long.

We got up early the next morning and drove to within a half mile of Fullers Cave, where the road ended. From there, we hiked up an abandoned fire road until we heard water pouring into an opening. We had arrived. Even though I had been there many times, I was always excited but also apprehensive when I entered the cave, perhaps because of previous challenging experiences there and just plain bad vibes emanating from the cave walls.

We got suited up, and I could feel the cold air rushing out as we began to work our way down into the sinkhole. Just before we reached the bottom, I sliced my finger on a piece of broken glass. It pierced right through my leather glove. I pulled off the glove, and there was a red drop of blood on the tip of my finger. Was that an omen? Maybe, because we had no idea what awaited in the darkness.

On this trip, it turned out we could get only two drysuits for the weekend. We couldn't find any wetsuits, so all we had were two suits for the four of us—unfortunate since we would be in water a majority of the time. At one place, after rappelling the first waterfall, we had to get off on a ledge and then swim across a pool to reach the next falls. The water was extremely cold, necessitating the proper equipment for us to keep warm enough.

Since we only had two suits for the four of us, we decided we would divide into two teams. Bill and Gene would be the advance team. They would go in with ropes and the cable ladder and rig the waterfalls by clipping our carabiners onto the existing expansion bolts so the rappels would be prepared for Marty and me. We would be the push team wearing the drysuits.

Marty and I decided to wait and meet them an hour later at the waterfalls. We would conserve our strength, check our equipment and packs, and then start into the cave. By the time we got to the waterfalls, they would have the ropes in place, and we could begin our rappel. Bill and Gene planned to turn around and head back out of the cave. They would be cold from having gotten wet in the falls.

When Marty and I reached the top of the waterfalls, we found Bill and Gene waiting at the bottom. They were pumped up and feeling great, even though they were soaked. They assured us that they felt able to go on with us for a while instead of heading back.

Together we retraced the path the previous expedition had followed to get to the rock breakdown that blocked the passage. I could hardy get my breath as I squeezed myself under the boulders. Like Bill, a month earlier, I was lying on my back in the stream, helmet and light off, my face pressed up against the rock, gasping for the least little bit of air. It was about the worst I have felt in my life.

When I crawled out on the other side, there was a big passage leading into darkness. We continued ahead, and I remember we had to climb some really steep, hairy mud banks and we were wading in water some of the time. Soon we heard a thundering ahead and popped out into a huge room. It was even more awesome than I had expected. The guys had describ-ed it when they returned home, but to look out now into a room with our carbide lights and not be able to see the other side or the ceiling was unnerving. It was like we had arrived at the center of the earth. We had no idea what was out there in the void until we had climbed up a massive mud mountain. It was just incredible.

We looked down at the bottom of the mountain and saw the river on one side and could barely make out rocks on the other side because of a mist rising from the rapids. There was just blackness beyond.

We sat there awhile, real excited. Then Marty and I presented our plan. "We're going to head downstream for as far as we can. We'll try to be out of the cave at around the twenty-hour mark from when we came in."

Bill replied, "Man, I am so pumped up I can hardly stand it! I am feeling so good, and I'm not too cold. I believe we can go down with you for a couple of hours and then turn around."

Gene added, "Yeah man, we can do it."

Marty and I questioned, "Are you guys sure you can make it?"

They confirmed, "Yeah we can make it." They were tough guys. Bill was a construction boss and had a hundred men under him. He was a real tough guy—an iron man. Gene was lean and in top-physical condition. So all four of us climbed back down the mountain, trudged along the banks of the river, scrambled over boulders, and splashed through the water.

When we came to the end of the enormous room, we found ourselves in a passage about fifty-feet wide. We could barely see the other side with our lights. We went around a bend and came to a lake. This discovery completely surprised us. We had expected this passage to go on for miles. Instead, there was before us a lake.

It struck me, when I first saw it, there was something weird about it. A yellow foam was floating on the surface. The ceiling was flat, about seven feet above the water. Its sides curved straight down into the water, which looked deep. By shining all our lights together, we could see the far end of the lake. There was no opening or outlet above the water. It was a spooky place. I had been exploring caves for years, but there was something about this place that was just scary. I don't have a rational explanation for why it felt so ominous.

About this time, Bill let out an incredible oath. Bill could tie together more cuss words than I knew. I thought I had heard it all in my college days, but this rant went on for so long he had to stop occasionally to take a breath. There was something really important he was trying to say. When he finely wound down, his voice quivering, he stammered, "This is what Paul dreamed!"

We asked, "What are you talking about?"

"This is what Paul told me about yesterday afternoon when I was loading up the equipment. He told me about this place!"

"You're crazy, man!" we interrupted. "Nobody has ever been here. You know that!"

"I know that," he replied, "but he had a dream about this place!"

I argued, "Well, how can you have a dream about some place where nobody has ever been before?"

"I don't know, but he described this lake perfectly."

The chills ran up and down my spine. Bill was obviously upset. The more he described the dream, the more we realized we were in Paul's dream. At that point, we looked down at our feet. We were standing on a crescent-shaped sandbar!

This totally freaked us out. We couldn't understand what was going on, but it was something really weird and mysterious.

Bill announced, "Let's get the hell out of here!" There was no argument. It didn't take the rest of us more than a second to realize that this was thing to do.

We wheeled around, took one last look at the ominous lake, and quickly headed back up the river. Arriving at the big room, we scrambled up the mud mountain.

Bill repeated, "We gotta get out of here!" Caving was what he lived for. He worked hard all week, and every weekend he went caving. It was the main thing he always talked about. This cave was the most intriguing cave he and the rest of us had ever been in. "We gotta go," he repeated. "Now!!"

Well, Marty and I thought about it, and Marty said, "Look, we're fired up, we're ready to explore, we've got on our drysuits, we're warm, we've got a lot of energy, we're ready to go. We can't go downstream because of the lake, so we'll just go upstream. We'll follow the river. We'll see what's there and plan to be out in about twelve hours."

I remember Bill's pleading, "Don't do it! There's something wrong! Don't do it!"

I finally said, "Well, *we're* going to do it! You and Gene can go out and wait for us."

They left. I remember we were sitting up on the mountain when they started making their way down. We could see their lights fading farther and farther away. We could tell when they walked across the river and finally disappeared into what seemed from our distance like a little hole but was 25-feet wide. For us, it suddenly grew very dark. There were now just two of us. We glanced at each other for a second, swallowed hard, and said, "Let's go caving!"

We climbed down the mountain and started upstream. There was no chance of getting lost as long as we stayed with the river, so we were not worried. As we began to walk along the edge of the river, it wasn't long before I began to have a bad feeling that something was watching us.

Maybe you've had that feeling, alone, out in the woods after sunset or walking through your neighborhood late at night or going into your empty house when no lights are on inside. Many people have had that feeling: prickles running up and down the back of your neck and your hair beginning to stand on end.

The farther we walked, the more my feeling grew that some thing was watching us. We weren't alone. I thought to myself, 'Good grief, Ward, you're just psyched out. This is the biggest cave you've ever been in. You've been a part of the most incredible discovery you ever imagined; no one has been where you are right now. You're just psyching yourself out.' But I decided not to say anything to Marty about it.

After a while, we came to the other end of the big room, and once again we were in a huge passage, but we were headed upstream instead of down. I guess we walked about ten minutes before the bad feeling grew stronger. I kept trying to put it out of my mind, but without much success.

We sat down on a gravel bar along the side of the river. I can see that gravel bar right now, like I was there at this very moment. I can see every pebble embedded in the water because of what Marty said to me. He turned to me, and I won't forget his words as long as I live.

He said, "Rocky, I've just got the strangest feeling we are not alone here in this darkness. The feeling I have is that something is in here. Something besides us. Something that knows we are here."

With his saying that, I thought I was going to pass out. I forced out, "Oh my God! Don't tell me that!" And I could feel myself just quivering, and my hands began to shake. "Man, I've been feeling the same thing for the last twenty minutes."

"Well, what are we going to do?"

I spouted, "God knows! I don't know what we're going to do."

So we talked, and I said, "You know? I'll tell you what I think this is." This is sensory deprivation. We're excited. We're spooked a little. This water is so loud we can hardly hear anything well. It's misty and we can't see well either. We're experiencing sensory deprivation. Yeah, that's what it is. When your senses are challenged, your mind starts playing tricks on you. That's bound to be all it is."

"Yeah, you're right," Marty said. "That's got to be what it is." He paused. "So what are we going to do about it?" He answered his own question, "Well, let's go caving!"

I agreed. "Yeah man, let's go caving!"

So we stood up and started up the river. That sensory deprivation idea had lasted about two and a half minutes. 'Heck,' I thought, 'whatever it was, it was a bad feeling, which was only getting worse.'

Eventually, we came to a place where there was a big canyon passage on the left. It was high and narrow, and a significant stream was pouring out from it. We agreed it would be a great passage to look into sometime but not today. So we continued upstream.

But as we walked, I began to have that feeling again. The feeling in my gut grew stronger that something was there. It wasn't human, and it wasn't animal. It might be something alien that lived in the cave, and we were penetrating its territory. I carried those thoughts as we walked a little farther and then stopped.

"Rocky," Marty said, "I tell you, this feeling is really eating on me."

"Man it's really eating on me, too."

"Well," he asked, "what do you think we ought to do?"

I muttered, "I don't know. I don't know if we could go out and tell Bill and Gene that we got scared and wimped out came out. I mean, what kind of deal is that?"

"Yeah, we can't do that."

I added, "Besides, this is the greatest cave discovery we've ever made."

"Yeah, it really is; we've got to go on."

I echoed, "Let's get going!"

Pretty soon we came to a place where the passage was narrower and completely filled from side to side with water. It looked deep enough to be a lake. We could see that the only way to get through was to cross that evil-looking water, which had foam floating on it, like the first lake we'd encountered, and the water was really black.

Marty said, "Guess we're going to have to swim."

I sighed, "Man, I don't know. I just don't like the looks of that water. I don't think I'm going to swim in it."

He encouraged, "Yeah, come on. You gotta swim."

When you swim with an open flame on a carbide light, you have to dogpaddle and not splash. If you splash too much, the water will hit your light and put it out. Marty started off dogpaddling and trying not to splash. In addition to his helmet and light, he was carrying a heavy pack and wearing boots. His drysuit gave him some, but not much, buoyancy. He continued paddling, fighting with the foam. God, this was awful. When he was most of the way across. he yelled to me, "Come on."

Reluctantly, I eased myself into the water up to my neck and started dogpaddling. About half way out in that black water, I had a clear mental image of what lay beneath the surface: a claw, a bony claw, reaching toward my kicking feet, GRABBING me, and sucking me down. It didn't happen, not then, but I knew we had to come back later.

We climbed out on the other side and continued down the new passage. The feeling was getting worse. It began with the suspicion that with each step we were getting closer to whatever was there, like a spider spinning a web and waiting for the fly to blunder into it. I knew it was waiting, knowing that we were coming. If we didn't turn around soon and leave, it would get us! It was some unimaginable thing: some ancient entity that lived there. For us even to see it would be so devastating that we would not be able to stand the sight.

Marty and I didn't talk about our feelings any more; I guess we both realized that if we mentioned what we were feeling, it would scare us both so badly we would turn and run.

When we came to another lake, I moaned, "Man, I've about had it."

"Yeah," he replied, "I have, too, but let's do just one more."

We had been in the cave for hours after the other guys had left. I said, "I don't think I can across another lake."

He urged, "Let's do it, and then we'll turn around for sure."

I proposed, "Tell you what, Marty. If the lake gets deep enough that we have to swim, I'm done!"

Marty agreed. "OK, that's fine. If it gets to the point that we have to swim, we'll quit and turn around."

We started out in the lake, which had a smooth bottom that grew gradually deeper. First, we were waist deep, then chest deep. When it was neck deep, I croaked, "Man, I'm going to have to swim."

Marty said, "Let's go a little farther to see how deep it gets. If we have to start swimming, we'll turn around."

About that time the lake grew shallower. "Good grief," I said. "Even though it's a little shallower, I'm still ready to quit!"

I think he was, too, but neither of us would allow ourselves to turn around and give up.

Gradually, we left the lake. We found that the cave was different there. Instead of one big passage with the river running through it, we were in a large room with a low ceiling and big piles of rocks lying all around.

We could gradually make out openings among the piles of breakdown, but it was hard to tell where the room actually extended and how big it was. We weren't sure which way to continue. As a result, we wandered aimlessly in the room until we came to a fork in the river. One side approached from the left; the other, from the right through jumbles of rocks. It amazed us that the temperature of the two forks was markedly

different: one much colder than the other. We surmis-
ed that one had flowed underground a lot longer than
the other.

At that point, we decided to leave the room and its
streams. We were getting tired and knew it was a long
way back to the cave entrance. We had to cross rivers,
ascend the mud mountain, and climb three waterfalls
on ropes. So we decided this was far enough. It was a
hard decision because, although we had made an
incredible discovery, we felt sure there was more cave
to be explored.

Turning to head back, Marty noticed a small hole
on a side of the room. In a solid wall there was an
opening about six feet in diameter. He sighed, "Well,
that looks like an obvious lead to more cave. I'm ready
to quit, and I'm really tired, but let's at least look up
there just to tell those guys we found a passage that
continued, if it goes somewhere."

I said, "Look, I'm going to sit here and rest, and if
you want to go look in that hole, by golly, go look in it.
I'm staying here!"

That's a common thing to do when you're caving
with people you know well. You reach a place that has
not been explored, and if someone wants to check out
a lead off the passage, you might say, "Okay, you go
that way, and I'll go this way or stay right here. Let's
meet back here in twenty minutes." We had done that
many times before, but not in this cave.

I said, "Don't go further than ten minutes. I'll expect
you back in twenty. I'll sit there on that rock and relax."

Marty headed toward the unexplored passage, and
I sat on a flat rock about two-and-a-half feet high and
ten feet long. It made a good seat. I hunched over with

my head down and my arms on my knees. I was exhausted. It was totally quiet there. The stream was in another part of the room, and it was flowing slowly. It was much smaller here than down in the big room. In fact, it was so quiet that I could hear my heartbeat. At first I heard Marty walking, then his footfalls retreating in the distance, and soon there was silence.

I thought to myself, 'Ward, you dumb idiot, here you are not only physically and emotionally spent but alone.' Suddenly I heard an ear-splitting, anguished scream. And I knew, I KNEW that whatever thing we had been feeling and dreading had gotten him! I found myself standing, facing that hole in the wall, and yelling, "Marty, Marty, Marty!"

There was nothing. Silence. No answer. I felt like my feet were cemented to the rocks. I couldn't move! I knew my friend was in trouble, but I could not move. I just stood there yelling, "Marty, Marty, Marty!"

I don't know how long that continued, but after an eternity, I heard a trembling voice: "I'm coming out! I'm coming out!"

Back in the 1960s, there was a science fiction television show I used to watch called, *The Invaders*. It was about aliens from space who would come down to earth and get inside the body of your friend or your wife or your mother or father or your sister. The aliens always looked like someone you knew on the outside, but inside they were terrifying aliens. The only way to tell was at night when their eyes glowed green. It was a really scary show. I had loved it.

When I heard Marty coming toward me, the thought flashed through my mind: 'Is this Marty? It might look like Marty, it might sound like Marty, but is it really Marty? It was obvious I was just over the edge.

Marty finally stumbled from the passage looking like he had aged ten years. He was shaking. His face was as white as a sheet. He sat down on my rock panting. I asked, "My God, man, what happened to you? What happened?"

He pulled himself together and groaned, "I went into that passage about seventy-five feet as far as a little room. It looked like a dead end at first, but I noticed about an eight-foot climb to an opening. I thought I'd stick my head over the ledge and shine my light in that hole to see if it went anywhere."

He continued, "I climbed about half way up with just a few footholds and handholds. When I was about four feet from the floor, my light went out. One minute it was fine, and suddenly it was out. It just went poof, and there was nothing but darkness." Sometimes carbide lights will just go out, and we say "gremlins blowing." For whatever reason they just pop, and out they go. It's not a big a deal usually; you get used to that happening. You stop what you're doing, pull out your flashlight, turn it on, and work with your carbide light until it's shining again.

When Marty's light went out, he was hanging on little footholds and handholds several feet off the floor and was plunged into absolute and complete darkness. At that moment, from the corner of his eye, he saw it— a green, glowing thing! He screamed and fell to the floor. Lying there shaking, he stared in terror at that green alien thing glowing in the darkness. In a cave with no light, you're not ordinarily able to see anything. But this green thing he could see. He lay there paralyzed with fear.

Meanwhile, I was yelling, "Marty, Marty, Marty!"

Finally, he fumbled around and found his flashlight. We usually wore our flashlights as a second light source on a leather strap hooked around a belt over our coveralls. His flashlight was on his leather strap as usual. With trembling fingers, he flicked it on to illuminate the source of that green, glowing thing in the darkness. It was a rotting log, not an alien creature at all. He realized the log must have washed in from the surface. The fungus growing on it was phosphorescent and had glowed in the dark when his light activated it.

I was more relieved than Marty with the reassurance that the real Marty was sitting there. I was so blown out that every fiber of my being was screaming, "Let's get the hell out of here!" and was overjoyed and actually surprised when Marty hollered, "Let's go!"

We turned and raced back down the passage. It isn't practical to run in a cave because it's easy to trip over something, fall down, break a leg, or turn an ankle. We ran to the river as fast as we could, knowing it was hours back to the big room and hours from there to the surface.

We hadn't gone far when I got the feeling that if something touched me on the nape of the neck, I'd be gone. I would die from fear, if nothing else! When you start whipping around, looking for what's gaining on you in the dark, you're pretty much over the edge. It was like a bad dream of some horrible creature on my heels, and I was stuck in molasses. I couldn't escape it.

But this was no dream. It seemed like we couldn't run fast enough. On the ragged edge of sanity, we were both in panic mode. The roar of the water and the enveloping mist increased our need to be extremely cautious as we climbed over wet, muddy boulders and felt our way with our feet through black water so we wouldn't plunge in a hole or trip over a rock.

I don't remember much about that journey as we made our way back down to the big room and the mud mountain. It was several hours. I don't remember swimming through the lake with the foam on it. I don't remember wading through the lake that was neck deep. I don't remember any of that, going back. Utter fear I do remember. After some incredible length of time, which is now lost to me, we reached the big room and climbed back up the mountain. The view from the top was the only way we could spot the passage that eventually led back to the surface and to life.

At the top there was a square area of rock and clay that was flat. "Let's take thirty minutes and rest up here," I suggested.

Marty confirmed, "That's a good idea, man. We've got to do it! Let's take thirty minutes. We'll just lie here on top of this mountain and rest, then head out of here!"

We lay there on the clay, and it hadn't been more than a couple of minutes before I heard very distinctly above the roar of the water far below three loud ka—splash, ka—splash, ka—splash. Just like that. It sounded like something huge was splashing in the water. It was just up the river from where we had just come. Marty was so startled he jumped up like he'd felt an electric shock and yelled, "Did you hear that?"

I responded, "Yeah, I did!"

"Oh, my God!" he yelled.

Scrambling at full speed, we tore down the mountain. We waded out across the river. I would not let myself look upstream, from where that sound had come. I locked my eyes straight ahead to the passage in the far wall.

We'd entered the passage about 100 feet when my light grew dimmer and dimmer. The flame was approaching nothing. I said "Man, I've got to change the carbide in my light!"

Marty complained, "Ah man, not now!"

"Look, I can't help it," I insisted. "I've got to stop and refill the light."

To change the carbide, it usually takes about five minutes, at least, sometimes ten. You've got to extract a plastic bag to hold the used carbide, unscrew the bottom of the lamp, and use a knife or screwdriver to scrape the gray carbide residue from the lamp.

Sitting on the floor of the passage, I was holding the top of the light in my left hand and the bottom in my right hand. I was preparing to set down the top of the light so I could dump the used carbide from the bottom into the plastic bag. I remember this like it was yesterday. I can still see the little stream right in front of me, the far wall—everything as clear as day.

Down in that huge room just around the bend from where we had entered our little passage sounded an awful KA-BOOOOOM, like a ten-ton boulder had fallen from that unseen ceiling and crashed into the floor. It was as if the whole cave lifted up three inches and sat back down. I saw my entire life pass before me in Technicolor, for I knew I was going to die. I had never in my years of caving heard a rock fall that wasn't loosened by a person. But, this wasn't just a rock.

I don't remember dumping out the old carbide or putting the new carbide in. The next thing I knew, the light was up on my head, and we were racing up the passage. I don't remember the details of running up the passage, but I do remember when we reached the water barrier, I had to lie in the stream on my back with only an inch of air space and wiggle under the rocks.

I had figured when we got there—if we got there—we could pass through that squeeze, and the boulders would become a barrier between us and whatever it was down there that was after us. Everything in me was screaming that I had no right to be in its lair.

Somehow we passed through the water barrier, but I didn't feel any better on the other side. I knew Marty was feeling bad, too. I could see by the look in his eyes, but we didn't dare talk about it. We were still 8,000 feet from the entrance, and it was up hill every step of the way with three vertical waterfalls yet to climb.

We arrived at the lowest waterfall, a 45-foot sheer climb. The way we usually attacked a climb was up to a narrow ledge about three inches wide with only a few cracks to use as hand holds. We used no belay or pitons. We would work our way toward the falls, where the water whistled beside us and onto the rocks below. About thirty feet up, we would hug the bottom of the cable ladder, which was already rigged for the ascent.

It's a real hairy thing to climb because the ladder swings back and forth and is only six inches wide. You have to climb it by wrapping your legs around it to hook your heels on the rungs and hug the ladder to drag your body up.

Marty made it up with some difficulty. When I started up, I had climbed about twenty-five feet and slipped. I almost fell. If I had fallen, I would have died on the jagged rocks below. I managed to hook my left arm through the ladder and was hanging there, trying to regain my footing on the ladder, which was swinging around in the spray of the waterfall.

I yelled to Marty, "I can't do it, Marty. I almost fell off. I can't make it."

He called out, "There's a little bit of rope hanging here from the upper waterfall. I'll lower it down to you."

Luckily, I had learned how to tie a one-handed bowline around myself, so I could be on belay for the rest of the climb. But he admonished, "You know, you've got two choices; you can stay there and die, or you can climb up." Wise words.

"Yeah, that's about it!" I sighed as I got myself together and climbed up.

The next waterfall wasn't too bad. It was a cascade that meant we could use the rope as a handline. Then came the third waterfall. We swam across the pool, clipped our jumar ascenders onto the rope and began the climb. I don't remember anything about that. I obviously did it and must not have had too much trouble doing it.

We managed to reach the top of the third waterfall, from which it was still well over a mile to the entrance. Waiting for us were waist-deep potholes and narrow canyon passages. There was more water, numerous climbs, and it was tough: like climbing out of hell. We'd walk a little way and have to stop and pant. With no time to rest, we'd been in the cave at least twenty hours, and we were both completely exhausted.

At this point, we were struggling just to put one foot in front of the other with the awful apprehension of what still lay behind us. The fear in my gut was hard as a rock and washed over me in waves. We didn't talk. My dread was that something would catch us during our last few minutes before we left its realm.

It was then that I began to smell it: the outside world, the smell of leaves and grass and flowers. I had forgotten that this was spring. It's a very, different smell from the smell in the cave. Underground, there is a clean, pure air, but whiffs of spring suddenly told me we were close to the entrance. I saw cans and glass and discarded pieces of an old car, a few blades of grass, and realized, at long last, we had arrived.

We clambered up the side of the sinkhole like denizens from hell: covered with mud, exhausted, pitiful creatures. It was about four in the morning. There was a cold drizzle, and outside was black as pitch. At the top of the incline, we saw lights and heard whooping and hollering and screaming and yelling.

It was Bill and Gene. They ran down, grabbed us, and helped drag us up the last few feet. They had a miserable little fire, half burning. It was mostly just coals. Without even trying to take off our drysuits, we flopped down by the fire.

Bill asked, "My God, what happened?"

Marty started talking, and then I talked. But as Marty talked, I began to realize he felt the same thing I was feeling exactly. He, too, had feared the creature that was following us. He, too, had been convinced he'd never come out of that cave alive.

The great joy and liberation of coming out was suddenly no longer there. I couldn't imagine what was wrong. We were out but still dreading some terrible creature was close. We were on the ground only thirty feet from the sinkhole, with the cave close enough to hear water running in it. It was pitch black dark. That pitiful little fire was quietly illuminating faces that were not human anymore. The veneer of civilization was stripped away. What lay underneath was raw terror! We didn't look like men: we looked like wild animals.

We fell silent. All we could hear was the slight hiss of the fire and the sound of water pouring into the opening of the cave. That yawning hole to hell was right behind us with something lurking inside.

I heard a noise and looked at Bill, the great macho iron man. He was weeping. Tears ran down his cheeks, and he was shaking. He uttered words that I will remember to my dying day. Sobbing, he said, "Suppose, suppose we have only dreamed that we have come out of that cave and that any minute now we're going to wake up and find ourselves still down there." I felt like I was falling. I don't know what it is to go insane, but it must be something like that: sitting there in the rain, terrified.

Finally, someone said, "I'm going to my tent now, but I will not sleep this night."

Like pitiful slugs, we crawled into our tents and lay down, determined not to sleep. When I finally slept, if I had any dreams, I hope I never remember them.

DREAM LAKE SONG

We should never have gone back into that cave,
To be trapped there and drowned in a watery grave.
Was it just a bad dream?
At least that's how it seemed.
Dreams never come true. Only nightmares do.

I'm not scared to tell you that I was afraid
And I'm sure that my friends will tell you the same.
Was there something in there?
In the damp, misty air.
Coming after them and me. The dark is all I see.

I don't ever want to go back to sleep,
'Cause I'm not sure I'd wake up from the dream.
Is it heaven, is it hell?
It's impossible to tell.
I only know what I feel, and the nightmare is real.
I only know what I feel. The nightmare is real.

Composed by Ken "Harny" Harnage, 1997.
Based on a story told by Rock Ward about Fullers Cave, WV, explorations
before it became the Culverson Creek System.

YOUR STORY 3

Challenge yourself by choosing an activity that takes you out of your comfort zone. It could be volunteer work in a food kitchen or tutoring a school student who needs extra help and attention. You may get involved in an activity sponsored by an ethnic group other than your own or dare to become a part of a discussion with an individual who looks at life differently from you. You could also choose that thing you have always wanted to do but have not had the fortitude to do it.

Describe what you did and and how you felt about it:

ABOUT THE AUTHOR

Rockwell (Rock) Ward, a retired Presbyterian minister, is a graduate of Rhodes College and Union Presbyterian Seminary. After two pastorates in Virginia, he served as campus chaplain at Appalachian State University and Warren Wilson College. In addition to hiking and caving, Rock has a lifelong passion for astronomy. He owns his own rooftop observatory and has shared his love of the starry sky with groups ranging from children in summer camps to senior citizens. He and Marrion have travelled to Norway, Venezuela, Chile, Iceland, and Easter Island to view eclipses and other astronomical events. He has visited a number of countries either as a volunteer worker or a curious traveler. Currently, Rock is fascinated by the ancient phenomenon of Thin Places as well as researching the evolution of the cosmos.

Rock, eating a small alien he captured in Water Sinks Cave